The Case of the Karate Kitty-Nappers

™

The Case of the Karate Kitty-Nappers

By Jesse Leon McCann

SCHOLASTIC INC.
New York Toronto London Auckland Sydney
Mexico City New Delhi Hong Kong

ISBN 0-439-20654-5

Lyrics to Ace's theme song by Ron Alaveda.

Published by Scholastic Inc.

Designed by Keirsten Geise

12 11 10 9 8 7 6 5 4 3 2 1 0 1 2 3 4 5 6/0

Printed in the U.S.A.

First Scholastic printing, September 2000

Ace's Theme Song

Ace Ventura, Pet Detective
Alrighty then!
He can sniff like a dog
He's slippery as a frog
Ace Ventura!
Radar like a bat
He's a way cool cat
That's Ace
If there's a tail
He's on the trail
He's sooo! protective
Even if his brain seems defective
Ace Ventura, Pet Detective
He can roar back in time
'N' save a dino in distress
Ace Ventura
He'll squash an alien bug
Eeeeuuuuw . . .
What a mess!
Ooooo, Ace!
He's pesky as a flea
Stings like a bee
Swings like a monkey and . . .
. . . Oooo what a hunk . . .
He's Ace Ventura, Pet Detective
Ace Ventura!
Alrighty then!

Chapter 1

Pop!

An object flew out of the kitchen, and Spike dived out of its way.

Pow! Another zipped by, just missing the monkey's head. Again he was lucky enough to duck out of the way just in time.

Ka-bang! This time Spike was ready. He jumped up and caught the flying object in his mouth. He chewed it happily.

Ace was making popcorn!

All the animals were gathered around the TV to watch the Yo-yo Kitten special. Spike had a hat on with Yo-yo Kitten ears. Ruff the dog wore Yo-yo Kitten boxer shorts. Lola Iguana looked cool in Yo-yo sunglasses. Sitting fluffed up on couch pillows was Buster the crab — he had a Yo-yo T-shirt on, extra small.

Ace fit right in — his apron had a picture of Yo-yo on it, and the words *Kiss the*

Purr-fect Chef. He grinned. Today, the real-life Yo-yo Kitten herself was going to be on TV!

Yo-yo Kitten was *very* popular. Every year, millions of backpacks, folders, notebooks, wallets, and pens were sold — all with Yo-yo Kitten's picture on them.

"Eeeek oop, eeek!" Spike said as he munched on some popcorn. Not enough salt.

"*Shhh!* I want to hear!" Ace turned up the volume.

On TV a reporter stood next to a big sign with Yo-yo's face and Japanese writing on it.

"Excitement is building in Tokyo, Japan," the reporter was saying. "Fans have come from far and wide to attend the grand opening of the new Yo-yo Kitten Mega-Store."

A videotape of the real Yo-yo came on screen. Her face had been slightly scrambled digitally, so the viewers wouldn't see it too clearly. *That* was done on purpose.

"As most everyone knows, Yo-yo Kitten is unique," the reporter said. "She is so *unbearably cute*, no one can look directly at her. Anyone who *does*, just goes wacky!"

Ace nodded — he knew all about Yo-yo. Anyone who saw her would run around in circles, shriek at the top of his or her lungs, jump in a lake, or do other crazy things — all because she was just so darn adorable.

To make sure that didn't happen, Yo-yo had to be carried in a special silk-lined case. Her guards wore dark sunglasses with blinders. When she made an appearance like today's, she was kept up on the stage in the back, far, far away from the audience. Her owners, Yo-yo Kitten Industries, didn't want to take any chances. Even then, people reacted strangely. She was just *sooooo* cute!

The big moment arrived. The TV cameras panned to Toshiro Mo'yen, the president of Yo-yo Kitten Industries. He stepped up to the microphone to introduce Yo-yo.

"This TV screen sure is smudgy!" Ace complained. "I can hardly see." Ace grabbed Spike and used him to wipe the screen. "Ah, that's better!"

Spike was going to complain — but Yo-yo was about to appear!

They watched as a light hit the stage where Yo-yo's case sat. The crowd applauded wildly, then became totally silent. A guard approached the case, slowly slipped open the latches, carefully raised the lid . . .

. . . and it was empty. Oh, no! Yo-yo was gone!

Someone had kitty-napped her!

Ace looked around at his pet friends. Lola Iguana swished her tail with worry. Ruff let out a sad howl. Buster clacked his crab claws angrily. Spike had his face pressed up against the TV screen, sobbing.

"Don't worry, animal buddies. When there's an animal in need, Ace is on the case!"

Spike turned as if to ask, *What do we do?*

"Let's send a telegram," Ace declared.

The next afternoon, Ace and Spike were heading home from the Florida State Fair. As usual, Ace was driving with his head out the window. In the backseat were three baby pigs. Ace had won them in a greased-pig-chasing contest.

"Spike, my main-monkey-man — was I on, or was I *on*?" Ace puffed up his chest. "These little porkers will never be part of anyone's dinner plans!"

"Ooo, chee chee!" Spike agreed half-heartedly. He *was* really *im*pressed with

how Ace had corralled the slippery pigs at the fair. But he was still *de*pressed about Yo-yo being stolen.

"Instead of taking them home, what say we take them to our *office*, Spike? That way, grouchy Mr. Shickadance will never know about this little piggy, or that little piggy. . . ." Mr. Shickadance was Ace's landlord. And he did *not* like animals.

Spike nodded. It was a good idea.

Ace surveyed his office. He was excited about bringing the piggies to their new home. All his pets were busy doing their clerical duties. Clarice the chicken was pecking at the typewriter. She was typing out Ace's "to do" list. Rory Raccoon ran the fans, making sure the office stayed cool. Shep the sheepdog was dusting, while Conrad Cat cleaned the windows. Harvey Hedgehog stapled papers and Monsieur

Parrot answered the phone. Spike was in the back. Ah, yes! Everything was running smoothly.

Suddenly there was a knock at the door. With his feet up, Ace was sure it was the landlord, come to collect the rent. He put on a big grin and opened his door. "Yeeeeeeeeeeeees?"

Ace's eyes flew open wide. On the other side of his door was a giant office-building ogre bending down to get him!

Chapter 2

At least, Ace *thought* it was an ogre.

He screamed, jumped back, and threw his arms around Spike. Then he realized the giant ogre wasn't an ogre at all. He was just very big and round. And he wasn't bending down to get Ace. He was bowing. In Japan, that's how people say hello. And the big, round man was Japanese.

"Please pardon the interruption, Ventura-san," said a smaller Japanese man, who walked around the giant. "I hope my personal secretary, Mr. Sumo, did not give you too much of a fright."

"Not at all. I always like to show prospective clients that I'm light on my toes," Ace said, casually putting Spike down.

"My name is Toshiro Mo'yen of Yo-yo Kitten Industries," said the man. Ace and Spike were surprised to see the guy they'd seen earlier on TV. Mo'yen gestured to a

Japanese businesswoman who followed him. "And this is our vice president, Ms. Jasmine."

"Aloha," said Ace, bowing.

Mo'yen had received Ace's telegram offering his services, and had traveled to Miami in his private jet to hire him.

"Everyone in our country is so sad now they can't work. We must get her back!" Mo'yen exclaimed, teary-eyed. "I myself can hardly bear it!"

Mo'yen became so upset, Sumo had to lead him outside. Mo'yen did not want to lose face by crying in front of Ace and Spike. Jasmine stayed behind.

"So will you come to Japan and take our case, Ventura-san?" Jasmine pleaded. "We'll pay you . . . say, half a million yen?"

"Half a *million* yen, you say?" Ace's eyes got big. "Spike and I will be on a plane to Tokyo first thing in the morning!"

Ms. Jasmine thanked him and said good-bye. As soon as she was gone, Ace looked at Spike and did a big victory dance.

"Oh, yes! Yes! Spike, can ya feel it?!" Ace cheered gleefully. "Half a million yen! We're rich! We can retire to the Amazon, just like we've always wanted!"

Spike just frowned at him and crossed his arms.

"Spike, my scowling simian cohort, what is it?"

The monkey took out a foreign currency exchange book and showed Ace how much half a million yen was in U.S. dollars. It wasn't *that* much.

"Oh, ree-hee-hee-heally?" Ace said glumly.

At the airport, Ace and Spike had a problem.

"What do you mean you lost your ticket?" Ace demanded.

"Ooop! Eeep!" Spike replied grouchily.

Ace thought for a second. Then he

walked up to the airline ticketing agent and held up his ticket.

"My hairy little boy here, *Ace Jr.*, lost his ticket. You *know* how children are. You'll let him on anyway, won't you?" Ace gave the agent his biggest, friendliest smile.

The agent took a good look at Spike.

"Your son? I don't think so. If that's your son, I'll be a monkey's uncle!" he said seriously. "The chimp goes in cargo!"

"What?" said Ace indignantly. "Are you going to make *me* ride in the cargo hold, too? Because where my primate pal goes, I go!"

Later, sitting in the cargo hold, Ace had to admit it wasn't so bad. But Spike was mad because he was missing the in-flight movie and snacks.

They weren't the only passengers in the cargo hold. There were also several big animals heading to the Tokyo Zoo.

There was a lion, a Siberian tiger, and a panda bear. But the animals were a little sad about leaving their old homes.

Ace decided to cheer them up by leading them in an old-fashioned sing-along. He pulled out his comb and hummed into it. Soon all the animals were singing along with him. The mood in the cargo hold was much happier.

"You know what they say, Spike. Music soothes the savage beast!" Ace crooned, "Okay, everyone! 'Kumbaya,' one more time!"

"Ook, ekk, pah-toohey!" Spike sputtered angrily. Who did Ace think he was calling a savage beast, anyway! But even Spike had to relent after a while. He joined in the singing as the airplane flew west over the Pacific Ocean toward Japan, land of the rising sun.

Chapter 3

As soon as their plane landed, Ace and Spike were whisked off in a pink limousine with Yo-yo's face on the side. They headed straight for the new Yo-yo Kitten Mega-Store, where Mo'yen and Jasmine showed them the crime scene. Everything had been left exactly as it had been when Yo-yo was kitty-napped.

Spike dusted for prints. Ace sniffed around Yo-yo's case, working his nose like a police dog's. Suddenly, he snatched something from inside the case.

"Aha!" Ace exclaimed, holding up a tiny leaf. He stuck it into his mouth.

"*Hmmmm* . . . yummy! It has a familiar flavor, a hint of jasmine of the Asian variety, known for its eight-lobed corolla and double berries . . . but there's a subtle difference. I note the presence of the cherry blossom, also. The firm but less juicy flower of the *Bigarreaus* family. Interesting combination . . . and darn tasty, too!"

Ace put the leaf in his pocket.

"I'm not sure if this strange leaf is a clue or not," Ace declared. "But there's one thing I am sure of! The crime did *not* happen here. Everyone back into the limousine!"

"But how could you know that?" Jasmine asked, surprised.

"Yo-yo's scent in the case was very weak. She wasn't in there very long. Whoever took her did it mere seconds after she was placed inside," Ace explained.

"That means she was taken from my office," Mo'yen said.

"I had a dog and his name was . . . Bingo!" Ace declared.

At Yo-yo Kitten Industries, Mo'yen showed Ace and Spike a bank of video monitors.

"There are many security cameras in

the building," Mo'yen explained. "We record everything. If the kitty-napping happened here, you will find it on the videotapes."

Mo'yen gave Ace videotapes from the time in question. Then he left Ace and Spike to investigate. Ace popped the tapes into different VCRs and set them all to play.

As the videos ran, Ace and Spike saw Mo'yen entering his office. He was wearing a pair of special sunglasses as he carefully placed Yo-yo in the case, snapped it shut, then left.

Nothing happened on the screens for several seconds. But then a mysterious stranger appeared. He was dressed in dark robes and wore a mask. On the mask's forehead was a picture of an eagle's foot, a talon.

The stranger entered Mo'yen's office, opened the case, and took Yo-yo out! Yo-yo meowed softly and snuggled into the stranger's arms. The stranger closed the case and fled the building with Yo-yo.

"Alrighty then!" Ace said. "Now we know *how* it was done, and *where* it was done. Now all we need to know is *who* did it. But that's half the fun."

Suddenly, the masked figure appeared once more on one of the screens. Spike tugged Ace's arm and pointed.

"Back for more, eh?" Ace smiled. "Maybe this time he left a clue, or better yet, took off his mask."

Spike shook his head and tugged at Ace again, chattering rapidly.

"Ex-squeeze me, Spike. I'm trying to watch."

The intruder came to another room and stopped. He was looking at the back of a man who was watching TV. The intruder crept closer and closer, until he'd sneaked right up behind the man.

"Boy, Spike! That guy must be pretty stupid, letting someone sneak up on him like that," Ace said with a laugh.

Spike continued tugging at Ace's arm. He squawked as loudly as he could.

"Hey, look, Spike." Ace smiled, pointing at the screen. "That guy watching TV has a monkey just like you."

Spike smacked himself in the forehead. He slowly talked to Ace.

"What's that you say, Spike?" Ace said, trying to understand. "That *is* you on the screen? That's not a tape? And the stupid guy is me? Don't be silly! If that were true, it would mean the masked intruder was right . . . behind . . ."

Ace and Spike spun around just as the masked stranger zapped them with a stun gun.

"Put me . . . in, Coach . . . I'm ready!" Ace mumbled dizzily as he and Spike fell to the floor, fast asleep.

Chapter 4

"Ventura-san, are you okay?"

Ace slowly opened his eyes and looked up. It was Sumo.

"Gee-hee-hee, let me think," Ace said as he stood on wobbly legs. "No harm done."

But that wasn't true. After a quick search, Ace discovered that the security tapes were missing. The intruder had taken them.

Now the only clue left was the tiny leaf.

"If only I had access to a subatomic particle analyzer and a two-way video-phone," Ace said, examining the leaf.

"Why, Ventura-san," replied Sumo happily. "I have both in my humble office."

"Lead the way, my hefty host."

In Sumo's office, Ace called Woodstock,

his computer-genius friend in the United States. "Well, if it isn't Ace Ventura, pet shogun." Woodstock smiled as he appeared on the videophone. "*Konnichiwa!*"

"And a *Szechwan* to you, my cyber-samurai," Ace said. "I have something I want you to analyze."

He sent the data to Woodstock to interpret on his massive computer. Soon Woodstock had produced a full report.

"The leaf is a rare mix of jasmine and cherry blossom," Woodstock explained. "It's found only in a remote forest of Japan, five hundred clicks north-northeast of you."

Ace and Spike explored the forest for several hours, searching for the plant that grew the leaves. They stopped to rest by a small bridge — or *hashi,* as it's known in Japan — built over a babbling brook.

"Look, Spike!" Ace said excitedly. "It's a pair of *Andrias japonicus,* Japanese giant salamanders."

Sure enough, there were two cool-looking lizards lounging by the water. Each was about four and a half feet long.

"Good thing there're no chefs around! In Japan, they're considered quite a treat to eat," Ace explained.

The salamanders' eyes flew open. They jumped into the brook and wriggled away. Spike, hand on hip, frowned at Ace.

"Oops!" Ace slapped a hand over his mouth. "They must have heard me."

Only, that wasn't why the big lizards had fled. For, out of the forest ran three big, growling bears. They had long, dangerous front claws. And they were charging right for Ace and Spike!

Chapter 5

Spike squeaked and grabbed Ace's leg. Ace held up his hands. "We mean you no harm, forest friends!"

The bears didn't slow down.

"*Hmmm.* These are Japanese black bears, or *Ursus thibetanius,* Spike. You can tell by the furry white 'V' on their chests. They can be ferocious, but only if they happen to be in a bad mood."

Spike thought they looked in a *very* bad mood.

Then, the most amazing thing happened. The bears passed right by them.

Spike couldn't believe it. The bears had run under the bridge to hide.

"Something must have scared them," Ace said. "I wonder what?"

He didn't have to wonder long. Just then, a dozen strong men came out of the forest. They were dressed in dark brown karate outfits. They moved quietly, and each carried a bow and arrows. They quickly surrounded Ace and Spike.

The leader of the group sneered at the two friends. "We have lost the bears! How dare you interrupt our hunt!"

"How dare you interrupt my interruption?" Ace replied smoothly.

The leader stepped closer to Ace. "What are you doing in our forest?" he demanded.

Ace looked at Spike. "Not very friendly *and* bear poachers, too. Let me do the talking!"

Ace turned around, bent over, and grabbed his bottom.

"I don't mean to get *cheeky* . . . *butt* . . . where the bears are is not a *tail* I'm willing to tell, Mr. Grrr-*rump*-py!"

"What?! Are you making *fun* of me?!" yelled the angry leader.

"Gee-hee-hee-hee, let me think."

The leader was not amused. "Men, bind these prisoners. We will take them to our master!"

Quick as a wink, the men had tied Ace and Spike up and were carrying them away. Behind them, Spike could see the black bears watching from under the bridge. They looked grateful.

After a trek through the woods, Ace and Spike found themselves in front of a huge castle. The place was so well hidden, Ace and Spike didn't even see it until they were only a few feet away.

"This is the hidden *dojo* of our master, the Mighty Talon!" barked the leader. "You will tremble in the Talon's awesome presence!"

"Kooky! I love presents, don't you, Spike?"

Spike rolled his eyes skyward.

As they marched through a line of trees, Ace started sniffing. He stuck out his tongue and snatched a leaf off a tree. He munched. Then, he grinned.

"Spike, my mini–Magilla Gorilla, this

is the same kind of leaf we've been looking for!"

Inside the gates, there were many other men wearing karate outfits. They were practicing fight moves and breaking boards with their hands. As the hunters set Ace and Spike down, a loud noise sounded through the castle.

Gong!

The men immediately formed lines and stood at attention. An ancient bald man appeared.

"Bow your heads! The Mighty Talon approaches!" the old man announced.

All the men bowed as a figure in dark, flowing robes appeared. The Talon's face was hidden by a mask. It had a symbol on it — an eagle's talon!

Ace and Spike gasped. It was the same person they'd seen on the video screen — the kitty-napper!

Chapter 6

The Mighty Talon spoke quietly to the old man. The bald fellow turned to Ace and Spike.

"Why have you invaded our sacred territory?"

Now untied, Ace answered confidently. "O Mighty Talon! I heard of your *fab* dojo, and came to join-o you. I know karate, judo, and twelve other Japanese words!"

The Talon whispered to his spokesman.

"Ace Ventura and his assistant, Spike," the old bald man said. "Your reputation is known to the Mighty Talon. You will engage in a karate match. If you win, you may join us."

"Saucy!" Ace smiled. "There's nothing I like more than a little kung-fu fighting!"

"But if you lose, you will be thrown into the pit of endless pain!"

"Eh . . . no problemo. I *like* a challenge!" Ace started doing deep-knee bends. Spike gulped worriedly.

The old man clapped his hands. Instantly, Ace and Spike were handed karate outfits. Ace practiced his wild kicks and crazy chops. Spike wondered which one of the muscular dojo men would be first to beat Ace to a pulp.

Gong!

The men parted and Ace's opponent came out. Spike chattered and Ace turned white as a ghost.

The opponent was seven feet tall. He was so muscular, he was almost as wide as he was tall. His legs were thick and strong. His head was blunt and rounded, his eyes set wide apart. His claws were long and pointy, and he looked as mean as a bear.

Because he *was* a bear!

"Let us not fight, my animal friend," Ace tried to reason with the bear.

It didn't work. With blinding speed

and a loud snarl, the bear pounced on Ace, flipping him over and slamming him hard.

"Suuuuuure. Let's do everything *you* want to do!" Ace said as he hit the ground.

Spike tried to help Ace, but the bear grabbed the little monkey by his tail and threw him into the bushes. Then the bear turned Ace upside down and ground his head into the dirt.

Now Ace was angry. "That's it! *Nobody* messes with the 'do, *or* with my semi-faithful simian sidekick! *Hi-yaaah!*"

With that, Ace took a feet-first leap at the bear. But instead of kicking the animal, Ace jumped over him, plucking out one of his whiskers as he passed over him.

Ploink!

"Let's see that on instant replay!" Ace cried, leaping back over the bear. Once more, he pulled out a whisker.

Ploink!

The bear was furious! He kicked at Ace and swiped with his claws. But the bear was so mad now he couldn't concentrate. He kept missing.

That made the bear even angrier. He chased Ace all over the compound, then out the gates, then into the woods. Spike followed.

Ace let the bear chase him deep into the woods. Then he did a strange thing.

Ace stopped short, faced the bear — and let loose with a bunch of loud barking and grunting growls. The bear paused, confused.

Just then, three *more* huge black bears emerged from behind the trees. Ace had called to them for help. They surrounded Ace's opponent, growling at him ferociously. This bear was not one of them — he was a bully.

Ace's opponent was terrified. He was all alone, without his humans to back him up. He fled into the forest, leaving his karate suit behind. He was never seen again.

Chapter 7

"Loo-hoo-hoo-ser!"

Ace picked up the bear's karate outfit. He went over to the bears, rubbed their furry heads, and made bear noises. That was Ace's way of saying thank you. The bears were happy to repay Ace for saving them from the hunters.

Spike and Ace returned to the dojo. When everyone saw the bear's empty karate uniform, they were greatly impressed. Ace had won! The Talon reluctantly agreed to let Ace and Spike stay.

That night, Ace and Spike sneaked out of their room, which was in a separate building not far from the palace. They *had* to find Yo-yo Kitten. After avoiding several guards, they found an open window into the palace.

They quietly entered and searched the

palace. Nothing. Finally, they came to a closed door with two big guards.

"That's it, Spike. That's where they're keeping Yo-yo."

Spike scratched his head. How did Ace know that? Then Spike saw, too. The guards looked *really* happy, both with silly grins on their faces. That was exactly the effect Yo-yo Kitten had on people!

"I'll throw my voice and do a kitty impression, Spike. That ought to distract them."

Mewww! Me-ewww!

Ace sounded just like a kitty in trouble. Panicked, the guards ran down the hall to see if Yo-yo had escaped. Ace and Spike quietly slipped in.

"Quickly, Spike!" Ace said in a hushed voice. "Let's get Yo-yo and go-go."

But then Ace and Spike saw the world's most adorable kitten in the fur for the first time. Yo-yo was sitting on a pink silk pillow. She looked at them and purred. They melted. "*Awwww*. Isn't she the *cutest* thing you've ever seen, Spike?"

"*Ooooooh*." Spike had to admit she was. He was hypnotized.

Yo-yo licked her paw. Ace and Spike hugged each other. Yo-yo stretched. Ace and Spike squealed. Yo-yo flopped on her back and played with a ball of yarn. Ace and Spike jumped up and down, ran around in circles, and giggled like school kiddies. Gosh, she was cute!

Then suddenly, Ace and Spike found themselves surrounded by the Talon and his guards. *They* all wore special goggles, so Yo-yo's cuteness wouldn't affect them. The Talon quickly put Yo-yo into a box with no openings. The spell over Ace and Spike was lifted. Their smiles turned to frowns when they realized they'd been caught.

The little old bald man came forward angrily. "What are you up to?!"

"Relax, Popeye. I'll spill the spinach." Ace smiled and took a giant, deep breath.

"Yo-yo is the heart of Yo-yo Kitten Industries. With her gone, production comes to a standstill. So the Talon took Yo-yo before a big event, making sure everyone knew she was kitty-napped. However, the Talon made the mistake of leaving a rare leaf behind, which led us here. What everybody doesn't know is that Yo-yo is insured for billions of dollars, so even if Yo-yo Kitten Industries goes under, Yo-yo's owner will still be incredibly rich!"

Ace ran up to the Talon, grabbed the Talon's mask, and ripped it off.

"Isn't that right . . . Mr. Mo'yen?!" Ace yelled triumphantly.

Silence fell over the room. Ace looked at the Talon, his jaw dropping. The Talon *wasn't* the president, Mr. Mo'yen.

It was the *vice* president, Ms. Jasmine!

"Of course, I *could* be wrong," Ace said sheepishly.

Chapter 8

"Ventura-san, you were correct in *how* Yo-yo was stolen, but you were dead wrong about *who* and *why,*" Jasmine said, smiling cruelly. "Yo-yo has an unusually powerful cuteness. Think of what would happen if she were the size of a building."

Ace and Spike imagined it. It would be devastating! The whole nation would be so distracted by the adorable giant, no work would ever get done again.

And that, as it turned out, was exactly the plan! Jasmine explained how her scientists had invented a ray that would make Yo-yo grow over fifty feet tall. "We have big plans for Yo-yo. And you and Spike have arrived just in time to witness the transformation," Jasmine said evilly.

She pulled a switch. Immediately, a red beam was projected into Yo-yo's box.

"In twenty minutes Yo-yo will reach maximum size and I will release her upon

Japan. During the havoc that follows, my ninjas will take over the country!"

Jasmine and her men put on the special goggles. "My army will remain unaffected by Yo-yo," Jasmine said. "Before anyone even knows there's an attack, Japan will be mine!"

"Ree-hee-hee-heally?" Ace smiled as he fished a tiny two-way radio out of his pocket. "It just so happens, Sumo supplied me with this walkie-talkie to contact him if I found Yo-yo. He's heard every word you said. The police are on their way now."

Ace was right. Spike looked out a window. The police were busting through the main gate.

"What?! You deceitful man!" Jasmine shrieked.

"Why don't you cry about it?" Ace said smugly. Spike chuckled as Ace gleefully pointed at Jasmine. "Loooooooser! Ah-looooo, ah-zerrr!"

A battle royal began in the courtyard. Karate kicks and chops were being thrown everywhere. The dojo men were strong fighters, but the police were stronger. Soon the cops were inside Jasmine's palace, fighting their way up the stairs.

"It's all over, Jasmine," Ace said. "You might as well give up."

"Think again, pet detective!" Jasmine smirked, pointing at Yo-yo.

Under the red enlarging ray, the kitten had already grown to the size of a fat cat. Ace was mesmerized as Yo-yo busted out of her box. And she grew! — the size of a dog — and grew! — the size of a lion — and grew! — the size of an elephant! With his last ounce of strength, Ace quickly covered his eyes.

"Don't look, Spike! Quick, fetch us some goggles!"

Spike jumped up, grabbed the chandelier, and swung over two of Jasmine's guards, snatching away their goggles. Immediately the two men fell under Yo-yo's spell. They giggled and started dancing.

"It's too late, Ventura-san! Mighty Talon has won the day," Jasmine declared, just as the police burst into the room. She and her men had strapped rocket packs onto their backs. She held up a small ray projector. "And *this* is the only device that will return Yo-yo to her normal size. *Sayonara* . . . loser!"

"Hey! That's my line!" Ace yelled as he lunged for Jasmine.

But it was, indeed, too late. The ceiling opened up. Jasmine and her men fired their rocket packs and blasted off.

Ace and Spike glumly watched them disappear over the horizon. The damage was done. Precious Yo-yo just kept growing larger and larger. The police didn't have any goggles, and jumped up and down like giddy kindergartners.

Chapter 9

Yo-yo didn't stop growing until she was fifty feet tall. Then she jumped out through the opening in the ceiling and playfully pranced away through the woods. Ace and Spike grabbed a police car and followed her, making sure their goggles were on tight.

Once Yo-yo was out of their sight, the police returned to normal. The captain in charge radioed the army. Yo-yo Kitten was headed for Tokyo and should be considered very dangerous.

Mo'yen was upset. "Please don't let them harm Yo-yo!" he pleaded. But the captain couldn't make any promises.

By the time Yo-yo reached Tokyo, Ace and Spike had caught up with her. Spike chattered wildly when he saw what lay ahead. A line of army tanks faced Yo-yo — with their guns pointed right at her!

"I see them, Spike, my observant ape!" Ace said. "But I have a feeling all their *fire*power will be useless against Yo-yo's *cuddly*-power!"

Sure enough, as the army general was about to order the tanks to fire, Yo-yo started chasing her own tail. The general thought Yo-yo so delightful, he ordered his men out of the tanks for a look-see. Soon all the soldiers were laughing and hooting and jumping for joy. They waved good-bye good-naturedly as Yo-yo cavorted away. The giant kitten headed straight for the heart of Tokyo. She treated the city like a big playground all along the way.

Meanwhile, the people of Tokyo ran to the department stores to fill up on Yo-yo products. They grabbed Yo-yo stuffed animals by the armloads. They fought over Yo-yo notebooks and purses and posters and sweaters! It was a riot!

Subways stopped and hospitals closed. Stores and banks were emptied. Jasmine's men walked into banks, rolling away cart-loads of money. No one stopped them. Their evil plan was working!

Ace and Spike drove down the street in the police car, sadly watching the results of Yo-yo's charms. A house caught fire, and nobody came to put it out. The firefighters were too busy watching Yo-yo. The house burned to the ground. Luckily, the people who lived there were gone — they, too, had left to see Yo-yo.

Suddenly, Spike tugged at Ace's sleeve and pointed to a TV store. Jasmine's face was on every TV in the store window.

"People of Japan," Jasmine said, "if you want me to shrink Yo-yo back to normal size and stop this chaos, the government must turn over all its power to me!"

"Let's go, Spike," Ace said. "To the TV station!"

Jasmine and her men had taken control of the local newsroom at the TV station.

They knew the government would contact them soon if they wanted Tokyo to survive. Sure enough, the intercom buzzed.

"This is the prime minister," the voice on the intercom said. "I have come to turn over power to you. Please let me in!"

Jasmine smiled at the prime minister as he entered. He was a tall man, wearing a long coat and a big hat, with a fuzzy beard and dark glasses. He placed a piece of paper on the desk in front of Jasmine.

"Here is the document that gives you full power," said the prime minister sadly.

"But there's nothing on it!" Jasmine growled, looking down at the document. It did, indeed, appear to be blank.

"What do you mean?" asked the astonished prime minister. "It's written right there in black and white. Perhaps those goggles prevent you from seeing it."

Jasmine and her men took off their goggles. "No, the paper is still blank," Jasmine said, frowning.

"As blank as the walls of the jail you'll soon be in . . . looooooser!" The prime minister sounded a lot like Ace.

In fact, he *was* Ace!

Ace whipped off the long coat and hat he and Spike used to impersonate the prime minister. Spike had been under the hat, with his tail hanging down as Ace's beard. Both Spike and Ace wore goggles.

Spike jumped from Ace's shoulders and quickly grabbed everyone's goggles. Meanwhile, Ace activated a remote control. He had set up a camera on the building and pointed it at Yo-yo. Now, Yo-yo's face filled all the screens in the newsroom.

Jasmine and her men were immediately powerless. They were mesmerized by Yo-yo's spell. They stood cooing at the TV monitors. Ace snatched away the shrinking-ray device.

"I've said it before, and I'll say it again," Ace crowed. "Alllll-righty then!"

Chapter 10

Jasmine snickered.

She laughed partly because Yo-yo was wrinkling her nose in just the cutest way possible. But partly she laughed at Ace.

"You have *not* won, Ventura-san," Jasmine said between giggles. "Yo-yo has to stand completely still in the shrinking ray for *twenty minutes* for the ray to work, and she will not. After being in a box for so long, she is incredibly frisky!"

Ace looked at Yo-yo on the screen. Jasmine was right. Yo-yo was one big bundle of energy. She was jumping around, swiping her paws, smashing cars, and bashing buildings. Ace couldn't afford to wait until Yo-yo took a nap. Tokyo would be ruined by then!

"Come, Spike, my prehensile-tailed pal." Ace grinned bravely. "The city is in danger, and we're just the one-and-a-half people who can save it!"

* * *

Yo-yo Kitten frolicked down one of the largest boulevards in the city. She was heading toward Ace and Spike.

Ace and Spike stood their ground as the kitten's massive paws came closer and closer. Just when it looked like they would be accidentally squished by Yo-yo, Ace put his fingers up to his lips and whistled.

Tweeeeeeeeeeet!

"Come to me, my jungle friends!"

Suddenly, they were surrounded by animals. For out ran the lion, the Siberian tiger, and the panda bear that Ace and Spike had met on the airplane coming to Japan. Yo-yo had destroyed the zoo, and now all the animals were roaming the streets.

"Alrighty then!" Ace said, raising a pencil like a baton. "Let's sing a sleepy lullaby, softly and sweetly!"

The animals and Ace began singing. It was *very* soothing.

"In the city, the quiet city, the kitty sleeps today.

In the city, the peaceful city, giant kitty sleeps today."

Everyone on the street wanted to sing to Yo-yo. Soon a huge crowd was serenading Yo-yo in melodious, soft harmonies. Yo-yo sat down and yawned.

By the time everyone had reached the sixth chorus, it happened — Yo-yo had been serenaded into slumber.

Spike knew what to do. He aimed the shrinking ray at her. Twenty minutes later, Yo-yo was her normal kitty-size again. Ace gently put Yo-yo inside a box.

And so, the spell was broken. The people of Tokyo quickly returned to normal and began cleaning up the wreckage of their city.

Ace and Spike returned to Yo-yo Kitten Industries and gave the sleeping Yo-yo to Mo'yen.

"Oh, Ventura-san and Spike-san, how

can we ever thank you enough?" Mo'yen asked joyously.

"That's easy," Ace said, handing Mo'yen a piece of paper. "Here's my bill."

Back in their office in Miami, Ace said, "You know, Spike — when I write my memoirs, no one will believe that a kitten could cause so much trouble just by being adorable," Ace said, bending over the baby carriage where the three little pigs were sleeping.

They looked so cute in their baby bonnets, Ace got distracted and knocked a paperweight off his desk and onto his foot.

"*Ow!*" Ace said, hopping up and down on one foot. "Of course, I *could* be wrong."

Spike just had to smile.

Fun Animal Facts From the Ace Case Files

One Big Kitty — Siberian tigers are the largest of all cats. If they can't sing well, no one dares to tell them!

The Tall, Silent Type — Giraffes are the world's tallest mammal. They have no vocal cords, so they can't speak to one another. Talk about being seen but not heard!

The Biggest and the Noisiest — The blue whale is bigger than the largest dinosaur ever was and can be heard more than 500 miles away.

The Animal That Drives Ace Batty — That's right, Ace is not very fond of bats — but he should be. Bats can gobble up to 600 mosquitoes in an hour. With friends like that, who needs pesticide?

This Little Piggie Went to Market . . . Slowly — Humans have been known to raise pigs as far back as 9,000 years ago, maybe more. In those early days, only people in permanent settlements would raise pigs because they can't be easily herded over long distances like cows or sheep. Move it, you road hog!

Think Nests Are for the Birds? Think Again! — Gorillas move around a lot. When a band of gorillas comes to a new place, they each build a new nest for the night. They bend and weave leaves and branches into circular bowls about three feet in diameter.

If Only They Could Play Basketball — Male African ostriches have been known to grow as tall as nine feet and run at speeds up to 40 miles per hour. Watch out, Shaq!